The Great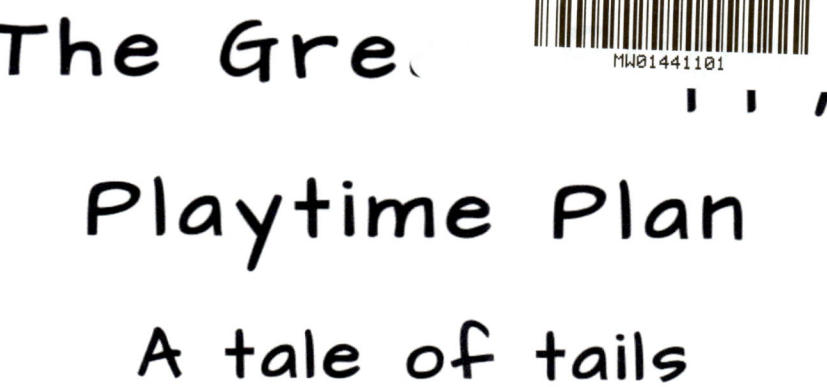
Playtime Plan
A tale of tails

author Gordon Lawry

About the author

Hello, I'm Gordon, a new Author and retired Navy Pilot. I am the father of two wonderful girls, that are grown up now. When they were children, I always delighted in seeing their faces light up when reading them classic books like Goodnight Moon, The Giving Tree, or Sleepy Ella. Their sense of joy and wonderment was what inspired me to pursue writing myself. I have always had a whimsical and vivid imagination but during my professional career in the Navy, I didn't have the time or the opportunity to explore any artistic inclinations. Now, as a new 'retired guy" I'm drawn to explore my artistic and literary side. My father was an artist and Air Force pilot. He actually excelled as a sketch artist before he joined the Air Force but after 38 years in uniform never returned to develop his craft further.

I enjoy writing in general and writing children's books for me has been the perfect creative outlet. Now as a Grandfather, storytelling has become a larger part of my life, as I am often entertaining my 5 year old grandson. I aim to spread the joy I see light up in his face, with children everywhere soon.

Preface

This book is dedicated to the memory of our two cats Yeti and Yoda.
Though we have had many pets over the years, few captured our hearts as they did.
Here's to Yeti and Yoda, the best of friends!
We would also like to thank our great neighbors Susan, Ray, Kathy, Ann, Toni, Dave, Jenny, and Jerry as well as their wonderful dogs for having Puppy Playtime every day and for inspiring this little story.

Gordon and Sandie

Hi, my name is Yeti and this is my best friend Yoda.

We were adopted as kittens and raised by our loving family, Chloe, Claire, and their parents, Gordon and Sandie. Sandie home-schooled the girls and after many years living next to the beach, we recently moved to a new neighborhood, and boy, do we have a story to tell you!

You see, Yoda and I used to eavesdrop on Chloe and Claire's home-school classes, so we also learned to read and write along with them!

I always hoped and prayed that one day our kitty reading and typing skills might come in handy and one day they finally did!

Every day Yoda and I looked out our window into our cul-de-sac and saw Gordon working on his beloved Volkswagen Camper bus and our neighbors taking their dogs for a walk.

The dogs looked happy to be outside, but they also seemed lonely.
We thought this was because the dogs never had a chance to play together.

The most fun they had was when the delivery man named Blake, on his shiny red bicycle, would came down the street and a dog would take off after him.

There was a total of five dogs in our cul-de-sac. First, there was the English Springer Spaniel named Lilly. She was all fun and always wanted to play!

Next was Tango, a little white Maltipoo with one heck of a bark! She fancied herself as the Alpha dog in the group and her small but mighty vibe commanded the respect of all the dogs!

Then there was Gustov or "Gus" as his owner called him. A very large, fluffy Berne doodle with an attitude that fit his size! Gus was big and lovable and had plenty of playfulness.

Next was Angus, another Maltipoo, and a natural escape artist! Angus spent a lot of time on his leash because he tended to take-off at the drop of a hat!

Lastly was Zac, the goofiest (and friendliest) dog in the group! Zac was a Labradoodle with a heart of gold, and a sweet, friendly disposition towards all!

One day, it occurred to Yoda and me that we needed to do something about the lonely dog situation in our new neighborhood. God says that we should love our neighbors as ourselves. So, we decided to hatch a plan! If we could just get the dogs outside at the same time to play, they would become best friends in a dog pack! But how? Just then I got an idea!

We would type out a personal invitation to each of the neighbors! The invites would ask each neighbor to come outside at four o'clock the next day with their dog. What a plan! Typing and printing out the invitations was a sinch because we had watched Sandie and Gordon do it many times before.

That afternoon while Gordon napped, I powered up his laptop and typed out the invitations which read "Please join us for a Puppy Playtime in the cul-de-sac tomorrow at four o'clock sharp." I hit print and made five copies; one for each neighbor.

I signed each invitation with a kitty paw print. Yoda had some fun tagging me with a few prints of his own!

The main challenge was, how to get the invitations out of the house and into the neighbors' mailboxes. Just then Yoda said, "Since I'm the stronger and sneakier one, I'll deliver the invites to the neighbors' mailboxes; just leave it to me!" Everything was going as planned when all of a sudden, Yoda picked up the all signed invitations and put them in the trashcan! I said, "Yoda, what in the world are you doing?"
He said, "Don't worry, this is how we'll get the invitations out of the house!"

Sure enough, Gordon got up from his nap, bundled up the household trash, and took it out to the street. Right on cue, Yoda started yowling for us to go outside and Sandie opened the door and let us out.

Quick as a flash, Yoda was head-first into the trashcan digging out the invitations. He had to stand on my shoulders to get them!

He then dutifully delivered the invitations to each neighbor's mailbox! Now all we had to do was wait!

The next day at four o'clock, all the neighbors and their dogs came outside and met in the cul-de-sac!

The very first Puppy Playtime dog pack extravaganza had begun!

There was a total of five very enthusiastic dogs! First there was Gus who took an immediate liking to Lilly who had her red dog toy and wanted to play "come and get me".

Then there was Tango and Angus running and barking at the top of their lungs. The two Multipoos were trying to get Zac to play with them, but he was happy and content to just be part of the excitement.

From then on, the dogs play together every day at four o'clock during Puppy Playtime and sometimes they even all get to chase Blake on his shiny red bicycle!

Our Puppy Playtime Plan to bring the dogs together was a huge success! The four o'clock Puppy Playtime has become a time-honored tradition that brings together the entire neighborhood!
As for the dog-pack, after chasing Blake on his red bike, getting into Gordon's VW bus seems to be their next favorite thing to do!

Gordon and Sandie attend Puppy playtime also, but Yoda and I prefer to watch and enjoy the fun from the safety of our window.

It turns out that loving your neighbor as yourself will bring you great joy, even if they are dogs!

Keep in touch!
Please join our mailing list for up-to-date information regarding discounts on my upcoming books and possible book-signing events in your area!

Go to

www.https://gordonlawry.com

for more information

or e-mail me at:

gordonlawryauthor@gmail.com

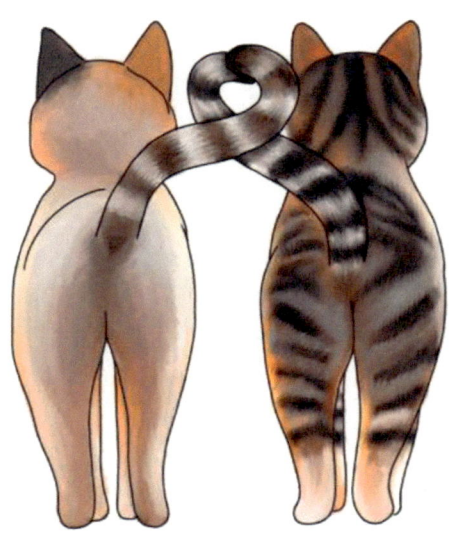

Made in the USA
Columbia, SC
07 September 2024